My Friend
Grandad

Written by Joshua George

Illustrated by Natalia Moore

IMAGINE THAT™

Licensed exclusively to Imagine That Publishing Ltd
Tide Mill Way, Woodbridge, Suffolk, IP12 1AP, UK
www.imaginethat.com
Copyright © 2018 Imagine That Group Ltd
All rights reserved
0 2 4 6 8 9 7 5 3 1
Manufactured in China

Written by Joshua George
Illustrated by Natalia Moore

ISBN 978-1-78700-605-8

A catalogue record for this book is available from the British Library

Sometimes Grandad comes over so I can look after him. Roger the dog comes too.

I try to keep them busy, but Grandad and I don't like any of the same things.

Grandad likes pushing.

But I like swinging.

Grandad likes taking
Roger for a walk.

But I like climbing trees.

Grandad loves Brussels sprouts.

I do not!

I do!

Grandad likes an afternoon nap.

But I like arts and crafts.

Grandad likes building.

But I like knocking things down.

Grandad likes following.

But I like leading the way.

Grandad likes
being the bad guy.

But I like being
the superhero.

Grandad likes reading.

But I like listening.

This story would be a lot better with a dog in it.

There is one thing that we both like ...

being the best friends ever!

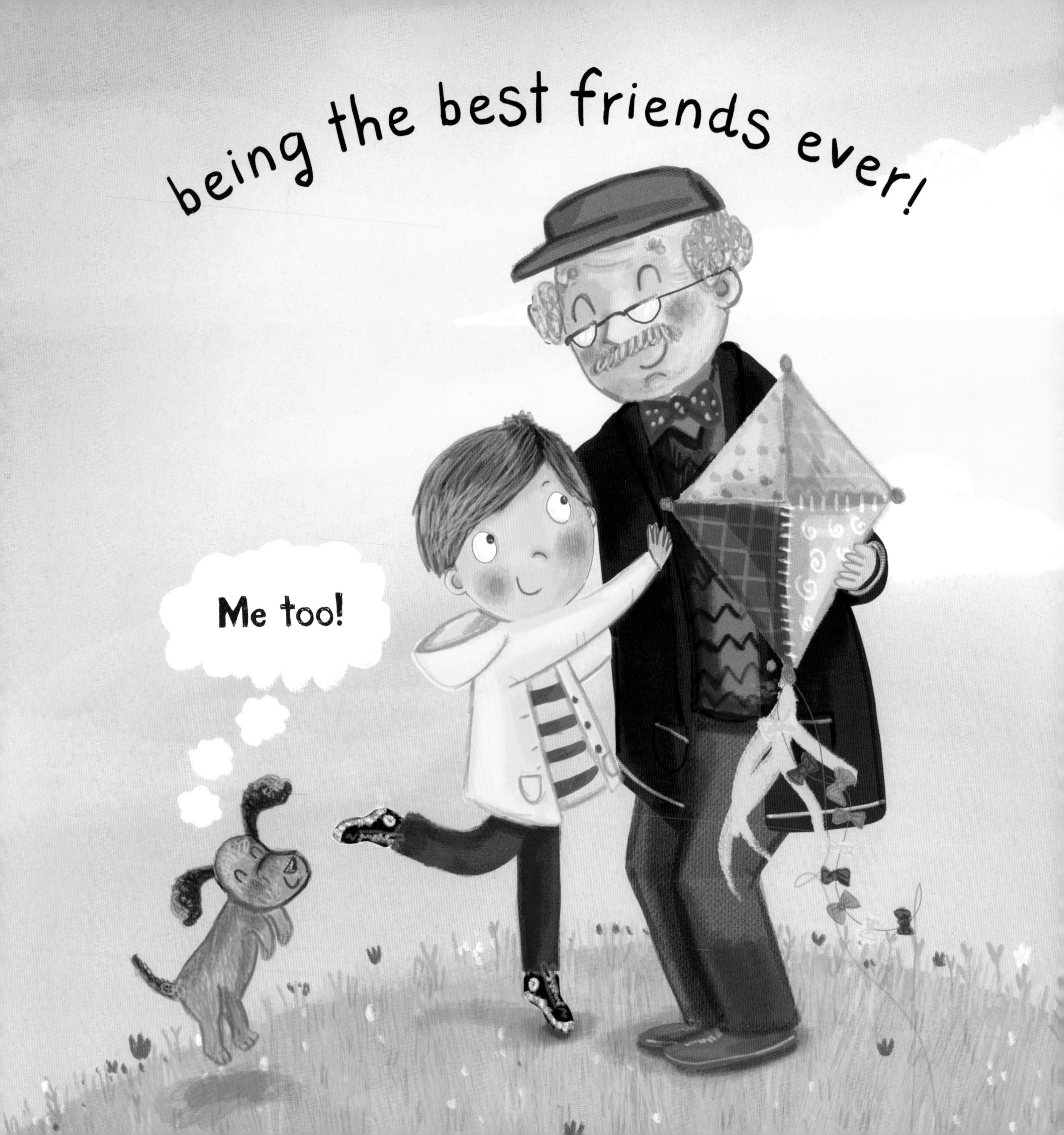